Whose EYES Are These?

Text and Wayne Lynch

WALRUS BOOKS

To Aubrey, the love of my life

Copyright © 2009 by Wayne Lynch

Walrus Books, an imprint of Whitecap Books

Edited by Paula Ayer

Photography by Wayne Lynch

Interior design by Warren Clark and Setareh Ashrafologhalai

Typesetting and illustrations by Setareh Ashrafologhalai

Printed in China

Library and Archives Canada Cataloguing in Publication

Lynch, Wayne
    Whose eyes are these? / Wayne Lynch.

ISBN 978-1-55285-992-6

    1. Animals--Identification--Juvenile literature.
2. Eye--Juvenile literature. I. Title.

QL949.L95 2009   j591.4'4   C2009-902691-0

The publisher acknowledges the financial support of the Canada Council for the Arts, the British Columbia Arts Council, and the Government of Canada through the Book Publishing Industry Development Program (BPIDP). Whitecap Books also acknowledges the financial support of the Province of British Columbia through the Book Publishing Tax Credit.

Canada Council   Conseil des Arts
for the Arts   du Canada

BRITISH COLUMBIA
ARTS COUNCIL

09 10 11 12 13   5 4 3 2 1

Humans have eyes that come in different colors. Some people have blue eyes or green eyes, and others have brown eyes. We use our eyes to see the world, but our eyes can also play tricks on us and make us think we see things that don't really exist, like ghosts or flying saucers.

Many wild animals have eyes that look very different from ours. Some animals have more than two eyes. Other animals have eyes on the side of their head or even on top of their head instead of at the front. See if you can figure out who owns the eyes pictured in this book.

I use my eyes to hunt for grasshoppers, crickets, beetles, mice, and small squirrels. My big eyes help me to hunt during the night as well as during the day. I usually live where the land is flat and there are no trees to block my view, so I can see a long way. When I stretch as tall as I can, I'm still shorter than a carton of milk.

Who am I?

4

I'm a burrowing owl and I live in the prairie grasslands of North America. Unlike most other owls, who live in trees, I live underground inside a burrow. A burrow hides me from my enemies and protects me from the hot sun in summer and the cold wind in winter. I often decorate the area around my burrow with bits of plastic, bone, paper, fur, and even animal poop.

If a burrowing owl gets trapped in its burrow by a hungry badger, fox, or coyote, it buzzes like an angry rattlesnake to scare the predator away.

I live in a world where it is sometimes very dark and sometimes very bright. In winter, it may be dark for many months because the sun doesn't rise. Then in spring, when the sun finally comes up, it can shine very brightly off the ice and snow. People wear sunglasses to protect their eyes from such brightness, but my pupils can constrict very tightly. My warm fur is brown in summer and turns white in winter.

Who am I?

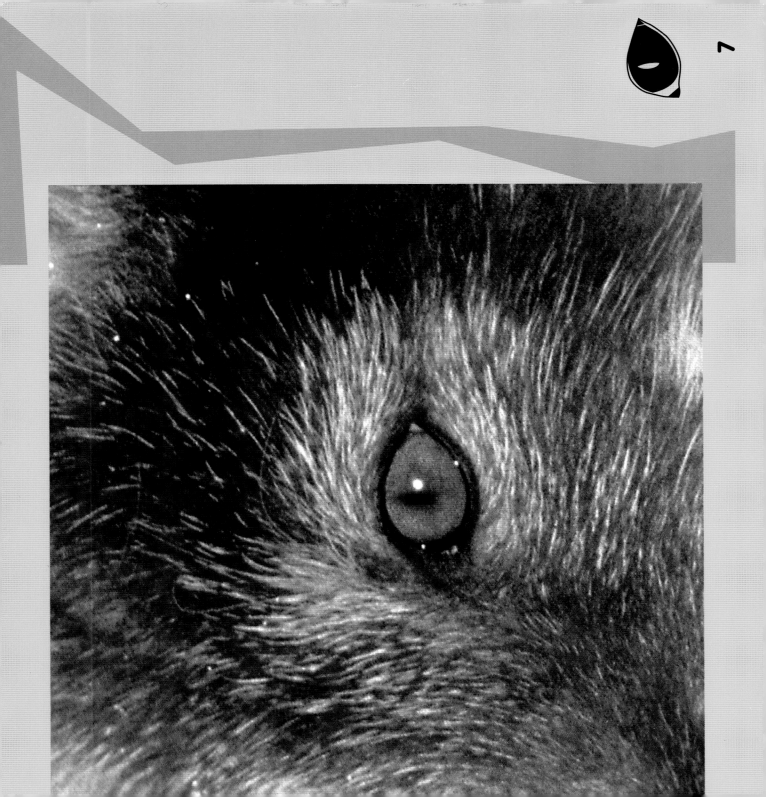

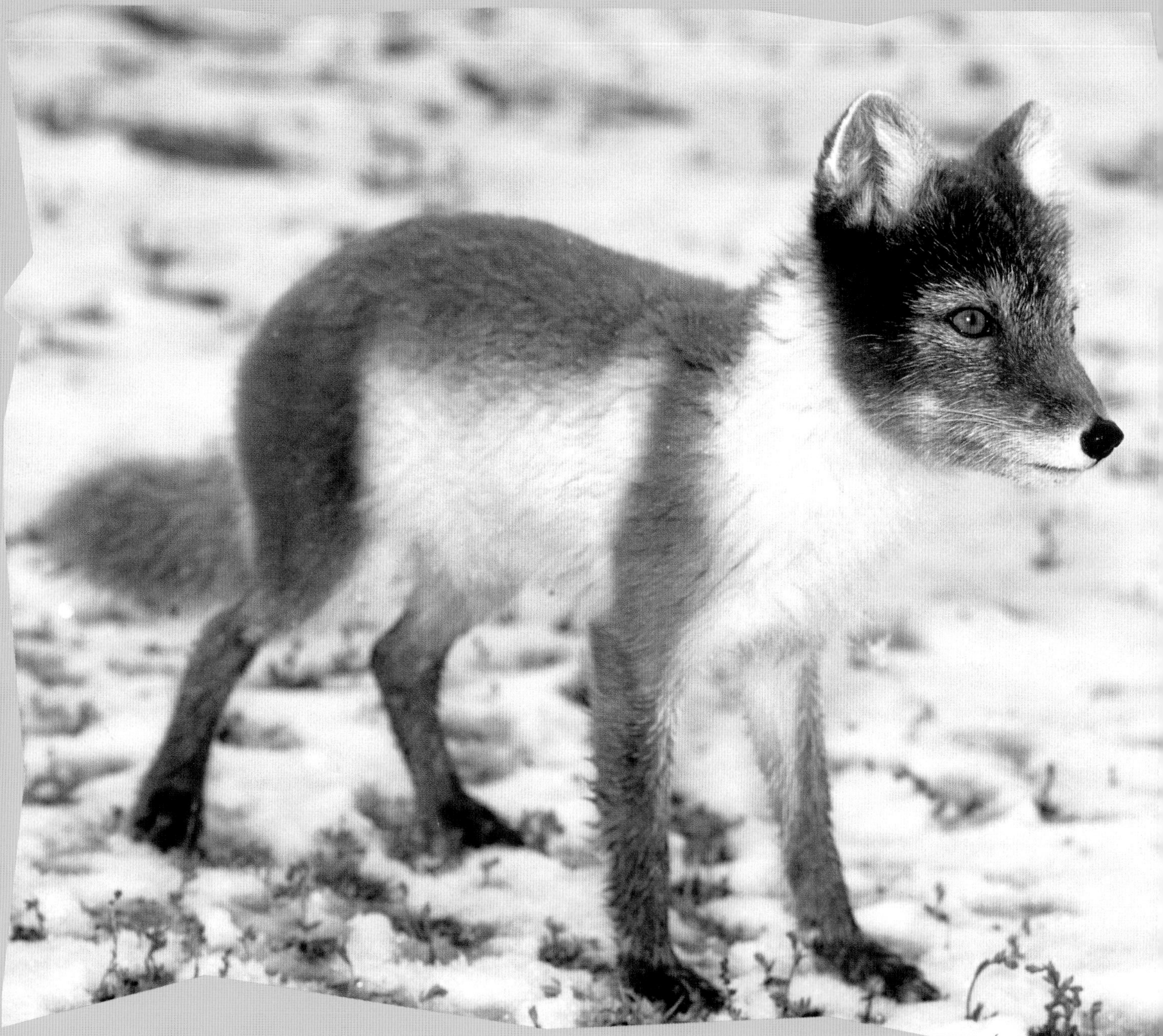

am an arctic fox. As you can tell from my name, I live in the Arctic, one of the coldest places in the world. In summer, I hunt lemmings, mice, and small birds. When there is lots of food, I hide the extra for later. In winter, I often follow polar bears on the frozen ocean and eat the leftovers from the seals that they kill.

A mother arctic fox can have as many as 11 pups at one time.

I have eight eyes, two on the sides of my head and six in front. I have two long teeth, called fangs, and I use them like needles to pump poison into the animals that I hunt. When I have babies, they ride on my back like cowboys on horseback at the rodeo. When it's time for them to leave home, they produce a silk thread and let the wind carry them away.

Who am I?

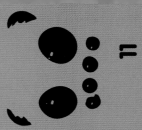
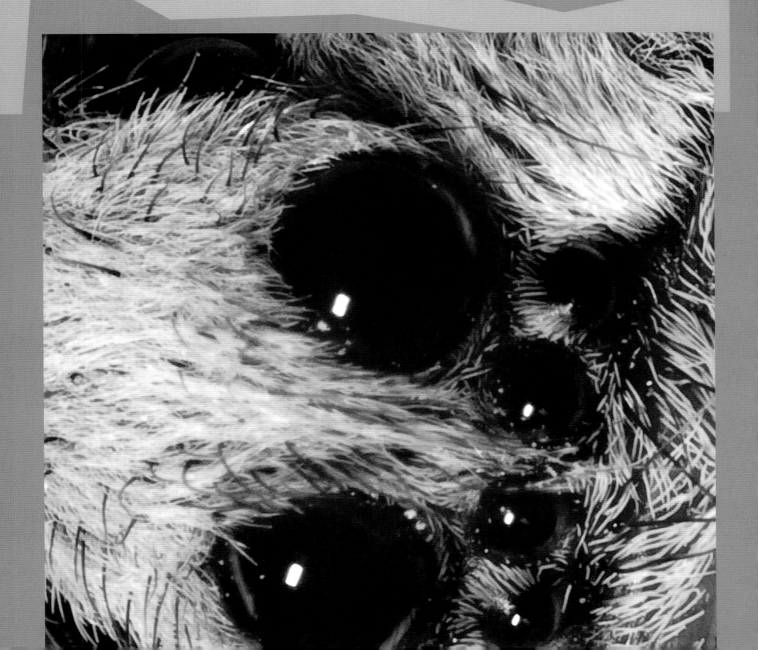

I am a wolf spider. I am a great hunter, and some people say I'm like a tiny wolf with eight legs. That's because other spiders build a silk web to trap their prey, but I hunt insects by running after them on the ground. My two big eyes and six smaller ones help me to see better than most other spiders.

A mother wolf spider can carry 100 babies on her back at a time.

I have really funny-looking eyes that sit on the top of my head and point upwards. With my eyes so high up, I can bury myself in the sand and still see everything around me. When I hide like this, I sometimes wiggle the tip of my tail above the sand so it looks like a tasty worm. When a lizard runs over to catch the worm, I catch the lizard.

Who am I?

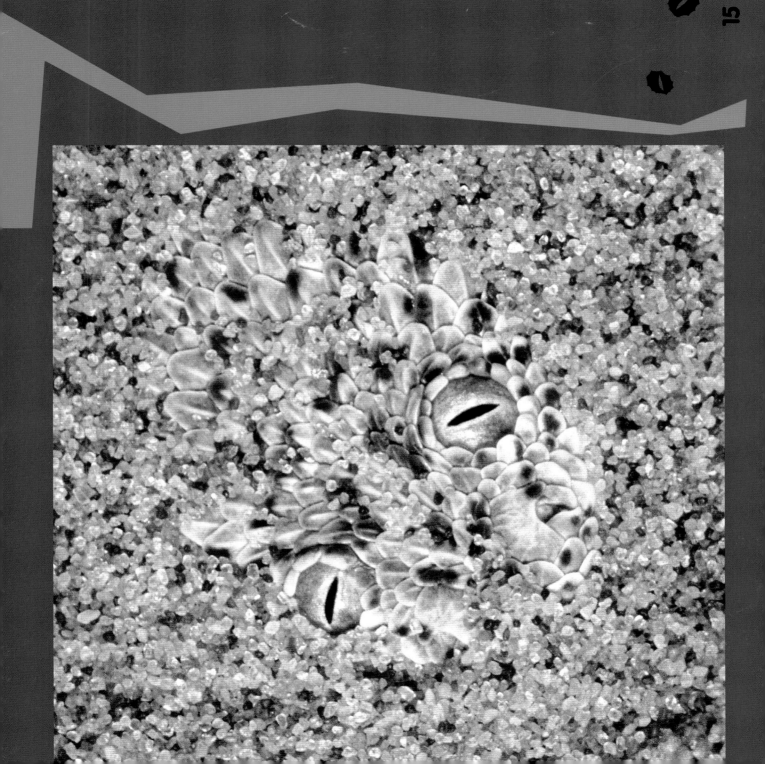

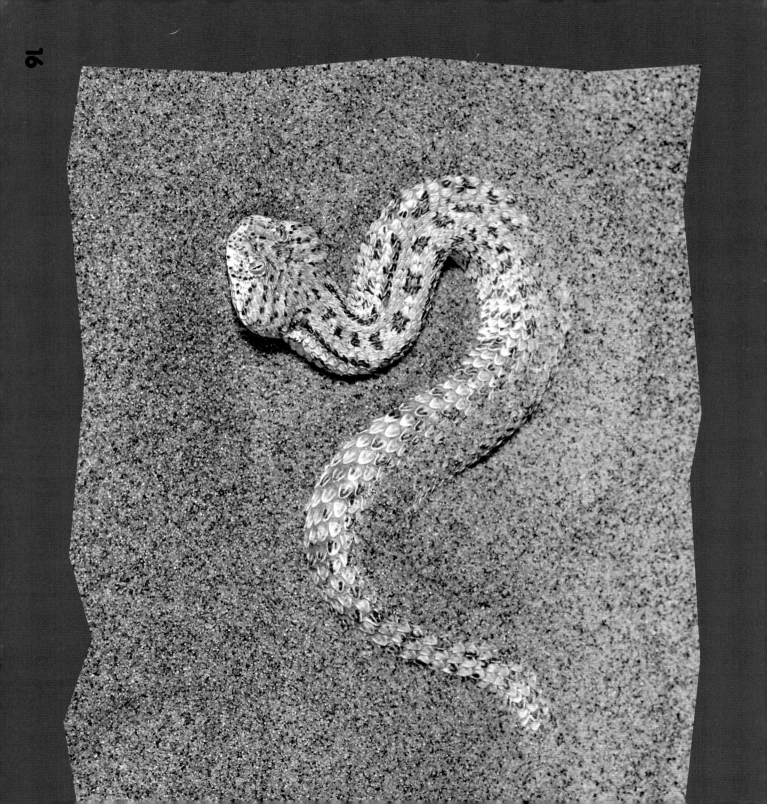

A sand snake can disappear under the sand quicker than you can count to five.

I am a sand snake and I live in the deserts of southern Africa. The sand in the desert can get as hot as a stove during the day, so I only come out at night. The desert is also a very dry place to live. At night, when the air cools down, drops of dew gather on my body. When I'm thirsty, I lick the dewdrops with my forked tongue.

Wildlife painters and photographers think I am one of the most colorful and interesting birds in the world.

My eyes are dark gray when I am young, but once I grow up they turn white. Other birds can see the white color of my eyes from far away. This lets them know how old and important I am, so they won't argue with me over food.

Who am I?

I am a king vulture and I live in the hot rainforests of South America. I eat mostly things that are already dead. That way, I help to keep the forest clean. The colorful skin on my face and neck gets brighter when I am excited or angry, in the same way that your face gets red when you are mad. The bare pink lump on my chest tells other vultures I just ate a big meal.

Vultures are very clean birds. They wash often in puddles and streams.

I live on the edges of lakes and rivers. When I am floating in the water, only my eyes and the tip of my nose are above the surface. My long, big body is hidden underwater. My eyes are especially good for seeing at night. Sometimes I may not eat for an entire year. When I finally catch a meal, I can stuff myself very full.

Who am I?

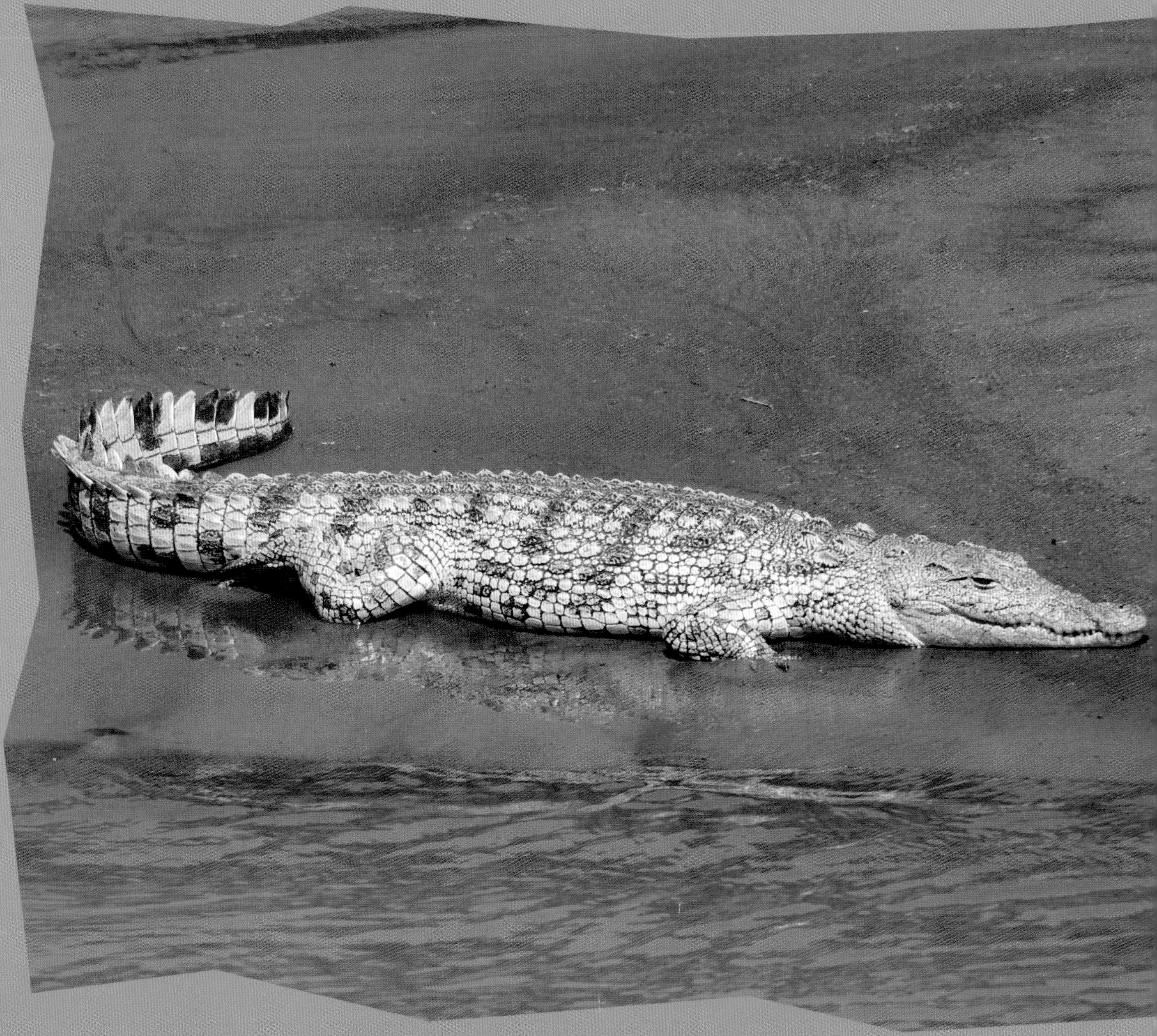

I am a crocodile and I live along the warm coast of Florida in the United States. I spend lots of time lying in the sun, like people do at the beach. But I don't want a tan. I need the sun to warm my body so that I can swim and move around faster. One thing everyone notices about me is my big mouth, which has 50 teeth inside.

A mother crocodile can lay 40 to 50 eggs in the sand. Afterwards, she guards them against egg-stealing raccoons.

I'm a noisy animal—some of my nicknames are "boomer" and "chatterbox." I use my sharp eyes to help me run, climb, and jump through the trees where I live. In the summer, I eat mushrooms, berries, seeds, and flowers, but my favorite foods are the seeds inside pinecones. Every winter, I store hundreds of pinecones in big piles so that I have something to eat when it gets cold and snowy.

Who am I?

I am a red squirrel and I live in Alaska and the northern forests of Canada. I live inside a hollow tree or build a nest out of sticks and leaves that can be as large as a big Halloween pumpkin. Inside the nest I'm safe from the dangerous hawks and owls that hunt in the forest. Like people, I'm busy during the day and then sleep at night.

A red squirrel can have as many as seven babies every year, starting when it is one year old.

Index